RILEY'S Remarkable Roller Coaster Ride

written by Emily Capuria, LISW-S
illustrated by Elizabeth Stryker, PT, DPT

Text copyright © 2023 by Emily Capuria
Illustrations copyright © 2023 by Elizabeth Stryker

All rights reserved. No part of this book may be used or reproduced in any manner whatsoever without written permission except in the case of brief quotations in articles and reviews. For information address B&T Publishing, 706 E. 185th St. Cleveland, OH 44119

ISBN 978-1-7329890-2-3

The artist used Procreate to create the digital illustrations for this book.

First Edition.

To Mac, always remember your magic.
I love you. Mom xox

To Abigail and Julia, thank you for sharing your magic
with me every single day! ES

Did you know you have a special magic inside?
To find it, we'll go on a remarkable ride.

We'll start by slowing our bodies' way down.
Let's take a big breath and see what can be found!

We'll go from bouncing all around and about—
Zigging and zagging, no calm throughout—

To peaceful and easy, so cozy and low-key.
Relaxed is the word that feels serene, zen, and free.

I'm ready to go—*are you ready too?*
To that magical place inside of you!

Your body is magic, so special and strong.
All that you need, you always carry along.

It's tucked right here deep inside your heart,
A magical treasure...there from the start.

Take a big breath in through your nose.
The air fills your whole body as up, up, and around it goes.

Through your nose, past your eyes, and over your brain,
Then down your back like a slow-moving train.

It sits at your heels for a moment or two,
Then give it a push to keep moving through.

Past your piggies it flows, to the tops of your feet.
It climbs up your legs as if they were a street.

Gliding by your belly button, swirling up your throat,
Finally to your mouth, and out, let that breath float!

This fun little breath is like a roller coaster ride
That unlocks the magic that lives deep inside.

Let's do this two more times, nice and slow.

In through your nose, up and around it flows,
Down your back and to your toes...

...now pause real quick before up and out it goes!

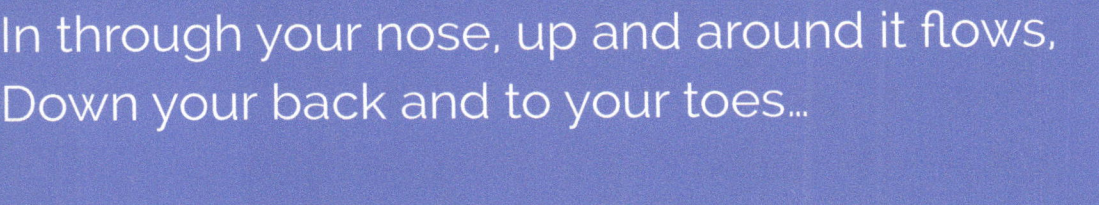

Let's take deep breaths and grow this calm more.
Relax your whole body and sink to the floor.

Now, with each breath, let your head settle down,
Feel your entire body melt to the ground.

Your breath opens that magical place inside
Where all your power and strength reside.

Exhale and relax.
I see you've got it now.
You're ready for the next step—
I'll show you how.

Start from the top where your hair meets your head.
Is it calm or prickly or something else instead?

Notice your eyebrows and chin, your mouth, and your lips.
How does it feel when your breath floats past your hips?

Feel your tongue and your chompers...
your ears, and your throat.
Open your mouth wide and yawn like a goat.

Just stop to notice—*that's all you really need*—
To unlock the power you have when you breathe.

Yes, you have a special power that's been here all along.
You can feel it when you breathe in deep and strong.

Hold on, wait a minute—*we can't be done yet.*
We breathe and we feel this magical breath.

Now as you breathe, pay attention, notice more:
Your elbows, fingers, heart, lungs, and belly for sure!

Breathe into your hips, legs, and booty too.
Breathe deeply through every part of you.

It's the simplest of things, like calming your body down,
That opens the magic that only in YOU can be found.

It's been there forever, and it won't ever leave.
To find it anytime, just notice and breathe.

How do you feel? Let's pause and check.
Think about your whole body for one quick sec.

Has anything changed on this roller coaster ride
That helps you relax and unlock the magic inside?

Notice your breath as it makes your chest rise.
It fills your whole body; there's so much room inside.

Breathe in and breathe out. You've got it—*way to go.*
You're amazing at this, I hope that you know.

Your body is powerful, mighty, and strong.
When you slow down and listen, it won't steer you wrong.

Your breath takes you to that magical place inside
Where you know who you are and don't have to hide.

You've relaxed your whole body. Here's a high-five!
Your lungs, nose, and belly—*everything went for a great ride.*

Your body is calm now, do you feel it so clear—
All of the magic that lives deep inside here?

There's one last thing I want you to know:
This breath and this body go wherever you go.

Anytime you need your magic, just close your eyes,
Take a breath, and feel your chest rise.

So cozy and calm, peaceful and relaxed,
You've tapped into your magic—*the code is cracked!*

P.S. I love you. You're amazing. Shine your magic bright!